Dr. Morris

W9-CSK-573

DISCARD

This book belongs to

ATHENEUM NEW YORK

For Garth

Also by Mary Rayner
Mr & Mrs Pig's Evening Out

LIBRARY OF CONGRESS CATALOGING IN PUBLICATION DATA

Rayner, Mary.   Garth Pig and the Icecream Lady.

SUMMARY: When Garth Pig tries to buy ice cream, he is kidnapped
by Mrs. Wolf, driver of the ice cream truck.
[1. Pigs—Fiction]   I. Title.
PZ7.R2315St   [E]   77-1647
ISBN 0-689-30598-2

Atheneum
Macmillan Publishing Company
866 Third Avenue, New York, NY 10022
Collier Macmillan Canada, Inc.

Printed in Hong Kong

First Edition

5 7 9 11 13 15 17 19   20 18 16 14 12 10 8 6 4

One very hot day Mother Pig was washing the kitchen floor.

The ten piglets called Sorrel and Bryony and Hilary and Sarah and Cindy and Toby and Alun and William and Benjamin and Garth Pig were outside playing in the garden. They had made a fort and it had been very hard work. They were all tired and thirsty, when drifting across the neighboring gardens they heard a faint *ting tong tingle tong*.

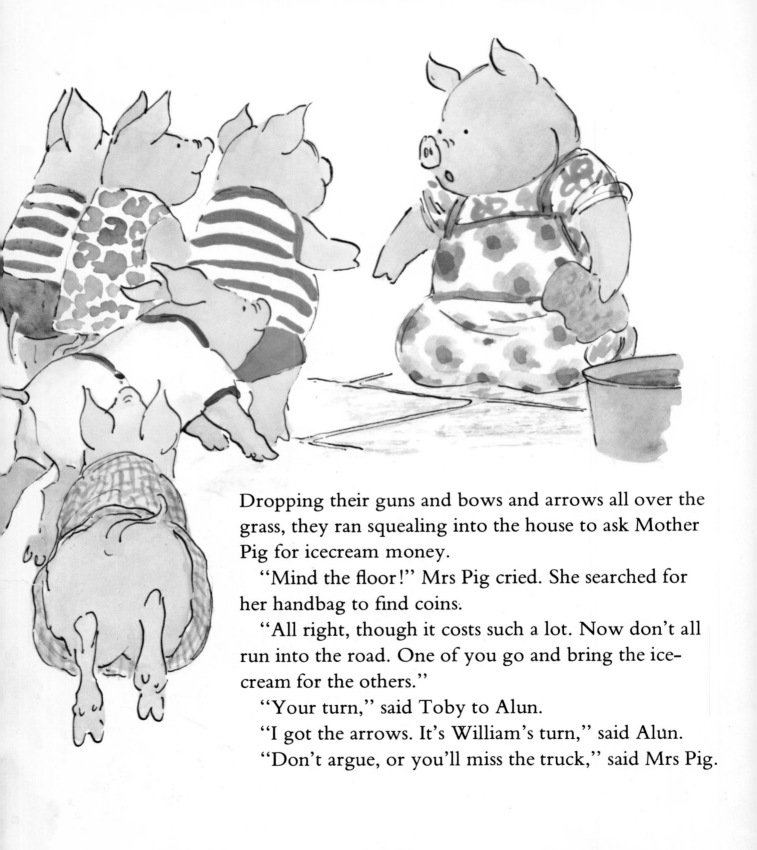

Dropping their guns and bows and arrows all over the grass, they ran squealing into the house to ask Mother Pig for icecream money.

"Mind the floor!" Mrs Pig cried. She searched for her handbag to find coins.

"All right, though it costs such a lot. Now don't all run into the road. One of you go and bring the icecream for the others."

"Your turn," said Toby to Alun.

"I got the arrows. It's William's turn," said Alun.

"Don't argue, or you'll miss the truck," said Mrs Pig.

"Quick," said William. "Stand in a circle everyone,"
and he began to count round:
Ham, bacon, pork chop,
Out you must hop.

Mrs Pig held up her trotters in horror and turned away
her eyes. "Goodness me, where do they pick up such
words? I am sure they have never heard them in this
house."

But none of the piglets was listening. Round and round they counted until only Garth was left. With the money clenched tight in his trotter Garth ran as fast as he could out of the house.

"Ten Whooshes!" they called after him.

The truck was parked down the road. It was a pink and brown *Volfswagon*, and written across the side in fat curly letters was *Lupino's Icecreams*.

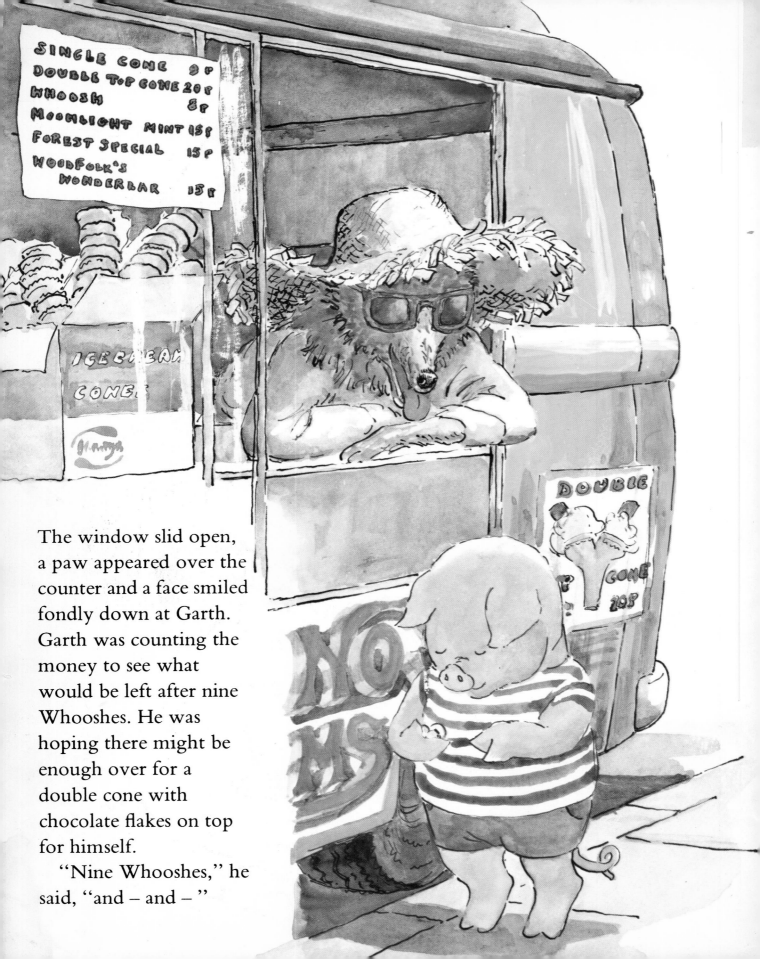

SINGLE CONE 9 P
DOUBLE TOP CONE 20 P
WHOOSH 8 P
MOONLIGHT MINT 15 P
FOREST SPECIAL 15 P
WOODFOLK'S
WONDERBAR 15 P

ICECREAM
CONES

DOUBLE
CONE 20P

NO ICE

The window slid open, a paw appeared over the counter and a face smiled fondly down at Garth. Garth was counting the money to see what would be left after nine Whooshes. He was hoping there might be enough over for a double cone with chocolate flakes on top for himself.

"Nine Whooshes," he said, "and – and –"

"Why don't you come up into the truck, my dear," said the icecream lady, "and see what's in the freezer?"

Garth trotted up the step and into the truck. As he leaned over the freezer the icecream lady closed the door and slipped behind the driving wheel. The truck began to move. It lurched off up the road carrying Garth Pig with it.

Meanwhile in the back garden the nine piglets were lying about on the grass waiting for their icecream.

"He is being a long time," said Sarah Pig.

"Probably dropped them," said William unkindly.

"Silly little pig," said Alun.

"Maybe he's eating them," said Toby.

The piglets looked at each other. It was a worrying thought.

"Better go and see," said Hilary.

They streamed in through the back door. Mrs Pig had almost finished scrubbing.

"Mind the floor," she said.

"But Mum, we're in a hurry," said Sorrel as they ran past, out of the front door and into the road.

There was no Garth. No truck either. Just a few blobs of icecream in a trail up the road. The piglets stood open-mouthed.

"He's been taken," said Sorrel. "Come on everyone, the bicycle."

Together they ran to the garage. Leaping onto the bicycle they swung out into the road and pedalled along the icecream trail.

But they had not gone far when they came to a cross-roads. There the spots of icecream petered out. The piglets came to a stop.

"Have you seen an icecream truck that goes *ting tong tingle tong*?" they asked a passer-by.

"No," she answered, "but one did go by which was going *snort squeal grunt grunt*. It went that way," and she pointed.

Far ahead the icecream truck had crossed the bridge and was climbing the long steep hill the other side, heading for the forest.

Inside the truck the driver
was singing softly to
herself:
*Fried or boiled, baked or
roast,
Or minced with mushey-
rooms on toast?*

Garth Pig heard her.
It was not a song about
icecream.

The road climbed up and up. The truck was going slower and slower, and the icecream lady stopped singing. There was a nasty smell of burning and the engine was making an odd uneven chugging. Then it stopped. The icecream lady left her seat and got out to look, but she locked the door behind her.

Trapped inside, Garth
Pig stood on tiptoe and
pressed his snout to the
window. It was very hot
in the truck. He peered
with his little pig eyes
down the steep grassy
slope of the hill, and far
far away at the bottom,
tiny in the distance, he
saw the family bicycle
toiling bravely up the
road.

Then he caught sight of the icecream lady coming back round to the door. He held his breath and ducked down. Now or never, he thought, watching the door handle turn.

As the door opened he bolted past her, dodged round the truck, and with a piercing squeal flung himself down the hillside.

Down the steep slope he rolled, as round and as smooth
as a barrel, gathering speed as he went.

The other nine piglets heard the squeal and saw him
bowling down towards them. Nearer and nearer he
came . . .

shot past and down and with a huge bounce came to
rest in some bushes near the bottom of the hill. With
one accord his brothers and sisters dropped the bicycle
and ran back down after him.

   William picked him out of the prickles and the
others gathered round. He was sobbing, "It's not an
icecream lady it's – " when they heard a terrible howl.

The bicycle streaked
down the hill, a frantic
figure clinging to the
handlebars. Not to be so
easily outdone, the ice-
cream lady had snatched
up their bike, but she
had reckoned without
one thing. That bike
was made for ten piglets,
not one lone wolf. It
hurtled past them, nine
pairs of empty pedals
spinning crazily, the
tenth held rigid by two
hairy feet . . .

swerved round the bend at the bottom and hit the parapet of the bridge. A dark shape sailed over the handlebars and fell with a tremendous splash into the river.

The piglets looked at the water. There was no sign of anyone. They looked up the hill to where the truck still stood.

"We still haven't had our Whooshes," said Sorrel. They scampered up the hill, Garth trailing after them. "Don't want a Whoosh, want a double cone," he whimpered.

Sorrel opened the truck door and went to the freezer. She handed out nine Whooshes, but when it came to Garth she paused.

"Here," she said, "there was enough money, I know there was."

She scooped out two gloriously over-flowing cones and putting a fat chocolate flake in each, gave it to him.

Then they all ran down the hill, picked up the bicycle, straightened the handlebars and rode home.

Next morning the truck was gone from the hilltop, but Madam Lupino was not heard of again for a very long time.